IT'S
GROUNDHOG DAY!

IT'S GROUNDHOG DAY!

STEVEN KROLL
illustrated by
JENI BASSETT

SCHOLASTIC INC.
New York Toronto London Auckland Sydney

To the librarians of Richardson, Texas,
who talked me into it

SK

ISBN 0-590-44669-X

Text copyright © 1987 by Steven Kroll.
Illustrations copyright © 1987 by Jeni Bassett.
All rights reserved. Published by Scholastic Inc.,
730 Broadway, New York, NY 10003, by arrangement with
Holiday House, Inc.

12 11 10 9 8 7 6 5 4 3 2 1   1 2 3 4 5/9

Printed in the U.S.A.   23

First Scholastic printing, January 1989

Summer was over. Godfrey Groundhog was getting ready for his long winter's nap.

He gathered lots of tasty green grass and hid it in his burrow. He mixed some straw with mud to make a mound to stop up his doorway.

When he was ready and the air was getting chilly, Godfrey invited his friends over.

"Friends," he said, "I've got a hunch. When I come out of my burrow on Groundhog Day, I don't think I'll see my shadow."

"Hooray!" shouted Sherwood Squirrel.

"That means we'll have an early spring!" said Penelope Porcupine.

"Six weeks less of winter!" said Reginald Rabbit.

Crouching behind a tree, Roland Raccoon was not so happy. "Hmph!" he said to himself. "An early spring means the snow will melt. I'll have to close my ski lodge. I'll lose lots of money!"

Godfrey Groundhog waved good-bye to his friends.
He stepped into his burrow and pulled the mound of
mud mixed with straw into his doorway. Then he got
ready for bed.

He brushed his teeth and put on his pajamas. He set his calendar alarm clock for 7:30 A.M. on February 2nd, Groundhog Day. Then he jumped under the covers and smiled as he went to sleep.

Up above, everyone but Roland Raccoon was talking about spring.

"If it's warm in February, we can go to the beach!" said Reginald Rabbit.

"Let's go buy some beach stuff!" said Penelope Porcupine.

"Good idea!" said Sherwood Squirrel.

While the three friends raced into town, Roland Raccoon went home to sulk in his hollow tree. "Hmph!" he said again. "I hate spring!"

Winter came. Snow fell. Godfrey Groundhog slept on and on. Sherwood Squirrel, Reginald Rabbit, and Penelope Porcupine went skiing at Roland Raccoon's lodge.

"Wheeeeeee! This is fun!" shouted Penelope Porcupine.

"Not as much fun as the beach!" said Reginald Rabbit.

"Skiing's better than the beach," said Roland Raccoon.

"Not when it's warm outside!" said Sherwood Squirrel.

Roland Raccoon frowned. He had to do something! He couldn't afford to have an early spring and warm weather.

Christmas came, and the friends had a party at Reginald Rabbit's. They gave each other presents and ate lots of good food. Then everyone went to Godfrey Groundhog's burrow. They sang a carol and left his presents in the snow.

At New Year's the friends blew noisemakers and wore funny hats.

"Happy New Year!" said Penelope Porcupine.

"Here comes spring!" said Sherwood Squirrel.

Up in a tree, Roland Racoon muttered, "Not if I can help it."

And then, before you could blink, it was February 2nd!

Promptly at 7:30, Godfrey's alarm rang. He reached over and shut it off. He sat up in bed and stretched. "It's Groundhog Day!" he said. "Time to get ready."

Then he opened his eyes. He was staring at a face in a mask!

"Help, a burglar!" Godfrey shouted. He dove back under the covers. Then he peered out again.

"Oh, it's you, Roland," he said. "What are you doing here?"

Roland pushed Godfrey Groundhog into a burlap bag and tied it with string. Then he pushed the bag out of the burrow and slung it over his shoulder.

Godfrey Groundhog kicked and screamed. "Roland!" he shouted. "What are you doing? Let me out! I have to look for my shadow!"

"That's exactly what I *don't* want you to do!" said Roland Raccoon.

Roland started home.

Godfrey wasn't heavy, but with all his kicking and screaming, he was difficult to carry. Before very long, Roland got tired.

He sat down under a tree to rest.

When he realized he was on the ground, Godfrey got right to work. He gnawed a hole in the side of the burlap bag and scrambled out.

But Roland saw him escape and ran after him. He tackled him and knocked him down.

He dragged Godfrey Groundhog the rest of
the way to his hollow tree.
He tied him to a chair.
Then he went to fix
himself breakfast.

As soon as Roland disappeared into
the kitchen, Godfrey began gnawing
at the ropes. He bit through one and
then another. He wriggled out of the
rest and started burrowing through
the floor!

When Roland came back, Godfrey was already burrowing into the ground. Roland started burrowing after him. "I'll get you, Godfrey Groundhog!" he shouted.

On and on went Godfrey. Faster and faster.

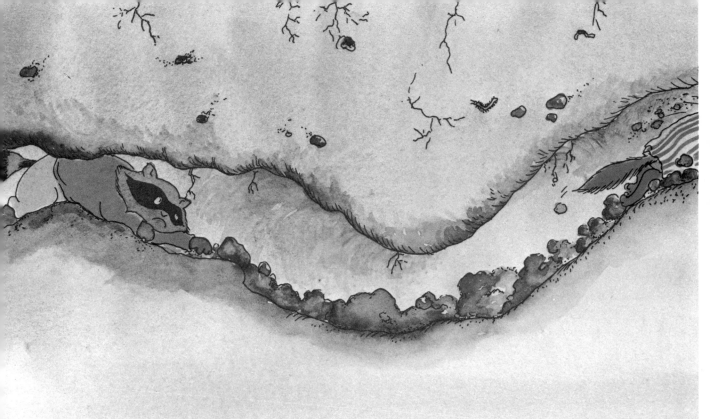

After so much breakfast, Roland could barely squeeze through the burrow. Every time he tried to go fast, he got stuck! Godfrey kept getting farther and farther ahead.

He raced toward home. When he arrived, he popped up next to his burrow.

His three friends were waiting.

"Where have you been?" asked Sherwood Squirrel.

"Are you okay?" asked Reginald Rabbit.

"We've been looking for you everywhere," said Penelope Porcupine.

"I was kidnapped by Roland Raccoon!" said Godfrey. He looked around. It was very cloudy. "Just as I thought. I can't see my shadow!"

Everyone got so excited, they forgot about the kidnapping. "Hooray!" they shouted, and danced around in a circle.

A moment later, Roland Raccoon struggled out of Godfrey's burrow.

Reginald Rabbit saw him first. "Get him! Get the kidnapper!" he shouted.

Roland dove back into the burrow, but Reginald Rabbit and Penelope Porcupine caught him by the tail. All four friends dragged him out and sat on him.

Roland Raccoon burst into tears. "I'm sorry," he said, "I just didn't want an early spring."

He explained about the snow and his ski lodge business.

"You can build a hot dog stand at the beach," said Sherwood Squirrel.

"But only after you're punished!" said Godfrey Groundhog. "You have to let us all ski free for the rest of the winter."

"I'll do anything!" said Roland Raccoon.

For the last weeks of winter, the friends had a great time speeding down the slopes.

Then they all went to the beach.